THE SIN EATER

D0994806

THE SIN EATER

Deborah J. Miller

SHORTLIST

First published in 2007 by
Sandstone Press
This Large Print edition published
2011 by AudioGO Ltd
by arrangement with
Sandstone Press Ltd

ISBN 978 1 405 62313 1

British Library Cataloguing in Publication Data available

Printed and bound in Great Britain by
CPI Antony Rowe, Chippenham and Eastbourne

Dedicated to the ladies of the SFF
Book Group:
Christine, Ali and Nikki.

With love and best wishes

CHAPTER ONE

The boy was lost. Most people would have tried to find a way back to safety, or looked for shelter and food. But this boy staggered through the shallow waters of the swamp, his white legs making a churning sound that seemed to echo his heartbeat.

Not that the swamp was ever silent. Birds, frogs and insects made the night come alive with sound. The waters flowed between the trees and islands of higher ground with a quiet lapping motion. Every now and then, a sudden louder splash meant that small crocodiles were hunting, pulling victims, deer or boar, from the shore as they knelt to drink from the still pools.

The boy was quite used to this, as the creatures of the swamp were the only living things for many miles. There were certainly no people. He could not remember how long he had been wandering here. He could not remember much of anything at all. His mind and body were burning with fever.

Some time ago he had been beaten, kicked and punched by a group of men. He could not remember who they were, but he could see their cruel faces snarling at him whenever he closed his eyes. He could still hear their curses and the dull thudding sound of the blows on his body.

They had wanted to hurt him badly, and they had done so. The burning pains in his chest must be from broken ribs. He had been coughing up bright wads of blood for the past few days. And yet, each time he visualised his attackers, what the boy could see in their burning eyes was not just hate, but fear. They had been afraid of him. This thought seemed ironic, almost funny, given his current condition.

Only one thick blanket covered his nakedness and he clutched it tightly around him with his thin white fingers, as if it were an embrace from a stranger. The blanket was stained with blood and mud from the swamps; bits of dead twigs and creepers had become entangled with it. At the bottom edges, the wool had become wet where it trailed in the waters, but the part around the boy's shoulders was merely damp. It seemed the only vague comfort in his confused world.

A bird, startled by the injured boy, took flight. It flew low across the water in the direction of the moon, its high call of alarm carrying far across the wasteland. The boy stopped and watched it go, his thoughts drifting. The bird was leaving the swampland so easily, just flying away. He wished he could do the same, but he felt quite sure he would never leave this place again. He felt numb and cold all the way through, as if he was dying from the core. Strangely, this thought did not upset him. His life would be no great loss to anyone, even himself.

He turned and lurched towards a nearby hillock, with the vague idea that he might get onto the drier ground for the night. Until now he had been unaware of seeking somewhere to rest. Perhaps he had not slept since he came to the swamp, or perhaps he had been somehow sleeping as he walked, a ghostly sleepwalker.

As he lifted his feet from the water, the boy realised his legs were completely numb. Once his brain recognised this fact, his legs refused to carry him any further. Throwing himself onto the prickly mat of the swamp-grass, he pulled himself forward, groaning aloud because of the pain in his ribs and chest. He had seen enough of the swamp crocodiles to know that he had to get away from the edges of the water. They were not large creatures but they could easily pull him back into the swamp to drown him, and then eat him at their leisure.

After a few agonising minutes he reached the top of the small hill and collapsed. Curling into a ball, he hugged his injured body tightly within the blanket. Then he must have passed out or fallen asleep. When he woke again it was night. He had no idea whether it was the *same* night, or if he had been out for a whole day. He was stiff and sore and he uncurled his limbs slowly, as if afraid they would break.

The pain was all-consuming now, his skin coated in sweat, his thoughts once again drifting like the fine mist floating across the surface of the water. It looked as if the hillock was adrift on an ocean of clouds.

Gazing out at the strange beauty of the place, the boy wondered why he had had to wake again—couldn't the gods have taken pity on him?

Couldn't they just have let him sleep forever?

His legs hurt too. As he looked down at his feet the first real reaction he had had for days broke through the blankness of his mind. Letting out a cry of horror he brushed at his legs with trembling fingers. Leeches had fixed themselves to him while he had been walking through the waters. Their slimy black forms, fat with his blood, were still attached to his flesh and glistened in the silver light of the moon. There must have been twenty of the creatures, one as long as his hand.

It was not easy to get them to let go of their meal. The first few that he tried to claw away burst open, covering his leg in bright, fresh blood. The smell was sure to attract crocodiles or other night hunters. For a moment, the boy's panic and despair almost overwhelmed him. He realised he was crying pitifully, and the movement of his weeping hurt his chest even more.

CHAPTER TWO

A sudden sound cut through his misery, forcing the boy to be silent. After a few moments he was unsure whether he had imagined it, or if it had come from an animal or bird. It was just that, for a second, it had sounded like a person—*another person in the swamp.* And that person had been laughing at him. He peered into the mist, his vision clouded by tears. Shapes seemed to move and drift there, teasing images that held their form for just a few seconds before falling apart.

The boy frowned. He thought he could see in the distance the ghostly outline of a woman, her hair waving in long floating tendrils.

'H—hello?' It was the first word he had spoken for days and his throat was so dry it emerged as a harsh whisper. But even as he spoke, the image of the woman whirled around swiftly to face him.

Then there was an unearthly scream, and she flew towards him, a hissing, flaming vision of hair and rags. The boy glimpsed jagged teeth and smelt her stagnant breath. With a yelp of fright he tried to pull himself backwards across the grass and banged his head against something hard. Looking round he saw the dark bulk of a tree-trunk, and pulling himself gratefully behind it, he peered round the side, his breathing coming in ragged gasps.

The vision of the woman had vanished, like a trick of the moonlight and swamp gases. He could smell the sharp fumes even now. For a moment, the 'ghost' had reminded him of someone and he tried to think who. But the thought drifted away, just as the woman had. It was like trying to re-capture the feelings and pictures of a dream. But he knew it was something to do with

9

her red hair.

'H-hello?'

He thought it was an echo at first, though it was minutes since *he* had spoken. But although the voice was imitating him, it sounded younger than he did—childlike in fact.

For the first time, he was thinking of something apart from his own pain. Although it was still bad, it had faded. It had become something in the background, like the frogs' croaking and the birdcalls. He frowned into the distance but the voice did not come again. Instead he heard the strange laughter he thought he had imagined earlier. It was a disturbing sound and it echoed around the empty skies of the swamps.

*　　*　　*

As he calmed down, the boy realised that the huge tree he had hidden behind was colder, more solid than wood should be. Peering at it more closely, he spoke only the second word he had uttered in days, and it was a curse.

The 'tree-trunk' was in fact a tall column made from black stone. It had an air of great age, although the carvings that covered its face were as clear as the day the stonemason had cut them. He felt he knew what the column signified, even though he had never seen one before. His weary mind searched for the word, then he tried to relax and let the word come to him.

Tauloc.

That's what it was—a Tauloc Tower. He remembered that they were created by the Shemari priests to mark the burial site of a wicked or restless soul. Or no, that was not quite right. The people buried underneath the towers were not always dead. Sometimes they were buried alive as punishment for terrible crimes. There must be a chamber here, underneath the tower, sunk deeply into the mud of the swamp. If he had had the energy the boy would have checked, digging his fingers down into the soft, wet earth, but it was becoming harder now to move because of the pain from his broken ribs.

Slumping at the base of the Tauloc, he closed his eyes. Even the night colours—the blues and greys of the grass, the bleached cream of the bulrushes—hurt his gaze. He was so weary that he could no longer cope with looking at the world.

The red hair. The girl with the red hair . . .

Had she been his friend? She had given him his blanket.

Kalia.

CHAPTER THREE

Now that he remembered her name, as he drifted into sleep, the boy could see Kalia in his dreams. And even though he was only dreaming, he could still smell the comforting musty dampness of the place he remembered as his home.

In the dream he could see Kalia standing right in front of him. Her lips were moving and it seemed as if she might be saying his name, but somehow, he could not hear the sound of the words. He could only watch as her mouth twitched up at the corners and her wide green eyes caught the hint of her smile. She was holding something towards him.

It was not the blanket—that came much later.

It was a small crockery pot with a stumpy handle. Food? Why would she have given him food? The dream felt so real and vivid that he was sure this must have really happened between them, in his past.

Looking around, he recognised they were standing within the cramped space of his tiny room. It was barely more than a cave really, burrowed out from the base of the hillside. Its uneven walls were held apart by a latticework of tree roots, which looked like black veins erupting forth from the broken skin of the walls and ceiling.

With this recollection of his surroundings, the sweet, familiar sound of Kalia's voice suddenly entered the dream; it came back to him like a returning wave.

'. . . and mother said that everyone who worked on the wall should get some food tonight, but you had already gone.'

His dreaming self, re-living this moment, now realises she seemed nervous or embarrassed that day.

She spoke quickly and a flush of colour spread across her cheeks.

'That's very kind of you, miss,' he replied, taking the pot from her outstretched hands. As he gripped the handle, their fingers brushed against one another and she pulled back quickly with a gasp, almost causing him to drop the heavy pot.

She turned quickly towards the door.

'Just bring the dish back to the kitchens tomorrow,' she said, her tone suddenly formal and aloof. Then, lifting the green cloth of her long skirt, she walked out into the darkness of the evening. It was raining outside, and a blast of cold, fresh air swept into the cramped space of the room, carrying the heady scent of her perfume back to him.

He stood still for a few moments, staring at the empty space in the doorway, as if she had turned him to stone. What happened, he thought? Could it be that Miss Kalia liked him, really liked him? He had no friends, *had become quiet and solitary since his parents died, and the idea that Kalia might care enough to bring him the food herself, rather than send one of the kitchen hands . . .*

In the dream, his thoughts were confused, but he moaned softly in his fevered sleep. He already knew the ending.

He was dreaming again that moment when he walked towards the doorway in a kind of trance. Rain was coming in through the gap, the droplets turning into long streaks of silver as they caught the moonlight. He put the pot down on the table as he went past and carried on to the door, meaning to close it.
As he reached up to pull the flimsy bolt across the top he heard low voices outside and, for some reason, their secretive tone made him stop to listen. They were female voices—young women of Kalia's age—and they

sounded breathless and scandalised.

'What did he say, Kalia? Did he speak to you?'

'Well, not really, he didn't say much, just 'thank-you,' Kalia replied. She sounded different when talking to her friends.

'I would have been too afraid to go in there.'

'You're so brave to go on your own. I didn't think you'd really do it. Your father would have him flogged if he knew . . .'

'Was he wearing clothes, Kalia? Because my brother says he's seen that boy walking around at night, stark naked! He's gone mad.'

The boy drew back, sensing they might glance towards the door. He could not tear himself away from their conversation, despite the sick feeling in the pit of his stomach.

'He was wearing trousers, yes.'

There was a slight pause before one of the other girls had breathed, 'no shirt then.'

'No.'

'Is he . . . ?'

'The same white colour? Yes. His skin is pure white, like a dead thing.' Kalia made no effort to hide the disgust in her tone. He thought she made it sound worse than it actually was, in order to impress her friends.

'Oh, poor you, having to look so closely.' A couple of them began to giggle in stupid girlish glee. After a moment, Kalia gave a small laugh too, although she sounded less amused than her friends.

He was stunned and sickened by their cruel humour. Reeling back from the door he grabbed hold of the pot of stew she had brought him. She must have done it as some kind of dare. His normal impulse would have been to hide away, but a dark ball of anger gripped his chest. Without taking any time to think, he just reacted. Yanking the door open again, he hurled the pot towards the girls with a yell of rage. The sound of it shattering against the trunk of the tree was followed by their thin squeals of fright. Gathering their skirts up they ran away, splashing through the puddles, laughing with excitement, uncaring that the boy had heard their spiteful chatter.

Only Kalia stopped. She turned and looked back towards the little cave. Her laughter faded from her eyes as she regarded the rough wooden door that had been firmly slammed shut. For a moment, it seemed as if she wanted to say something, to call out to him, but she did not. Her breath caught in her throat as she stood there, wavering. She didn't even seem to notice the rain, which was soaking her clothes to her body, and plastering her red hair against her face.

'Kalia. Come on!' one of her friends called back.

She did not move for a few seconds; perhaps she was waiting for the boy to show himself. It was impossible to tell whether that was so she could apologise, or taunt him further.

He had been watching her too, through a crack in the door. He stood as still as she, hardly daring to breathe. The colours of her soaking green dress and red hair seemed impossibly bright against the darkened shapes of the moonlit woodland. This image of Kalia was the one he would forever see in his mind when he let himself think of her in the future. When finally she turned to go, running to catch up with her stupid friends, the boy let out a long sigh. It was as if she had somehow released him.

His back slid down the wood of the doorframe, so that he sat on the cold earth floor, staring at the pale flesh of his own arms. He had always been so pale, always. But when his parents had still been alive people kept their thoughts to themselves. It was all so different now.

Somewhere in back of his mind, he knew that he was still dreaming. Even as he stared at his long white fingers against the blackened earth of the floor, even as he gave way to weak tears, he tried to force himself to wake up.

To wake up . . .

CHAPTER FOUR

The first thing he noticed when he managed to wake was that his pains had gone—not faded, but *completely* gone. And yet he knew this was quite impossible. The second thing he noticed was that someone was squatting down beside him, watching him with concern.

It was difficult to tell the age of the stranger, but he seemed young, possibly as young as twelve or thirteen. He had a striking appearance. Straight blonde hair stuck out from his head at crazy angles and his thin, delicate features had a clever, almost sly, look. The swamp mists still clung to his form, making the boy think this must be another ghostly trick of his mind.

'Hello,' the stranger said. He opened his eyes wide as he spoke as if showing surprise, as if he had just stumbled across the boy's body in the grass. He smiled, flashing perfectly even white teeth. Something about the way his smile turned up at the corners was slightly manic. 'My name's Spall. Seems you're sleeping on my grave.'

There was a pause as the boy considered all the possible answers to this introduction. Despite his pain being gone (he was sure this was something to do with the ghostly stranger) he was still bone-weary. His injuries and lack of food and water had left him in a state of exhaustion. As he stumbled for words, he closed his eyes again.

It seemed Spall was not very patient. 'Well, if you're not going to talk to me, I'll just go.' His tone was sulky and slightly teasing.

'No . . . I . . .' But it was too late, he was unable to summon enough energy or enough spit in his dry, cracked throat to answer Spall. This wasn't good enough for the stranger.

Even as the boy opened his eyes again, the ghost vanished, his figure cloaked by the mist until there was no sign that a person had ever been there.

The boy had been right, the mysterious Spall had magically been keeping his pains at bay in order to allow him to speak. Perhaps the young ghost was desperate for company. As soon as he had gone, all the pain surged back into the boy's body again, so that he let out a moan of despair.

'Come back,' he gasped. 'Please. Please.' As he curled into a ball once more he fought to focus on what the ghost had said to him. Not much really—just his name.

In his agony and despair, the thought came to the boy that in fact, the ghost had more hope of salvation than he had. He was still unable to remember his *own* name, even in his dreams. He knew that spirits and magical beings set great store by

24

such things. Maybe Spall would return and take his pain away again if he simply spoke his name aloud.

'Come back. Spall,' he moaned weakly. 'I c-can't tell you my name. I can't remember . . .'

'But I can.' Spall re-appeared, standing beside the boy this time. As his pain vanished again the boy managed to haul himself upright to stare at his strange saviour.

'Does being able to talk to you mean that I'm dead? Am I a ghost too?'

Spall smiled. 'No. Not yet. But you *will be* if I just leave you alone.' He seemed impatient: he had his arms folded and his long fingers drummed an irritable rhythm on his upper arm. 'Don't you want to know your name?'

The boy was beginning to feel much better. The main thing worrying him now was the fear that his pain could return. He stood up, his legs still shaky and weak, and peered more closely at Spall. He could still see the carved pillar of the Tauloc behind the ghost, right *through* the shifting colours of his body. The thought came to him that if he could simply keep talking to this strange spirit forever, he would never have to suffer again. Perhaps that was what the mysterious Spall wanted, a slave or a friend.

'Yes, of course. Everyone has to know their name. In fact . . .' he frowned. 'If I *was* a ghost, it would be the last thing I'd forget, wouldn't it? If I didn't know my own name, my soul would be lost. I mean, I'd never get to paradise.'

Spall nodded agreement. 'If you died right now—*if I let you die*—your soul would be lost forever,' he echoed. 'Unless I tell you first.'

The boy waited for a few moments, thinking the ghost must be about to tell him, but he did not. After a moment, Spall gave a boyish smirk. 'I'd be really, really grateful if you could do something for me in return, first.'

'So, you're saying that I *am* going to die. But you will kindly do me the favour of telling me my own name before I go? It doesn't sound like much of a bargain to me.'

Spall looked surprised by the speed at which the boy's thoughts had become clear. 'Don't you believe in paradise—in heaven? Or the gods?' His eyes narrowed suspiciously, 'you're not a heretic are you? Oh, great—that's just great!'

'No, no, I'm not a heretic. I do believe in the gods, although they seem to have no time for me. But it doesn't seem too bad to me . . . you know, dying and just ceasing to exist.' He shrugged. 'In fact, if you go away again, I'm going to die in agony anyway so death will be a release of sorts.'

For a moment Spall seemed stunned by the boy's fatalism. Then he had something of a tantrum. He stamped his foot in the muddy grass—though its ghostly form made no impression.

'Fine then, that's fine. You just— you just, die quietly, if that's what you want.' He turned as if to storm off, but then whirled back. 'And you can get off my grave-site when you do it! I don't want you here for all bloody eternity. Go on—get lost! Oh, here's your pain back. I don't see why I should make such an effort.' He pointed his hand towards the boy who was at once in agony.

The sudden renewed attack made the pain seem worse than before. The boy's body had no time to brace itself against the power of it, gripping him fiercely. He collapsed to his knees with a scream of despair.

Spall watched him writhe on the ground for a few moments, his face puzzled, as if he wasn't sure what to do next.

Eventually, he sniffed, 'your name is Sevim.'

Then he turned and vanished into the mist.

CHAPTER FIVE

The pain did settle down to become a kind of background noise again, as his body accepted it and his fever returned. He hunched by the edge of the water, knowing he was quite likely to be picked off by the crocodiles, but long past caring. His arms were crossed over his chest, holding onto his ribs to try and calm the movement of his breathing so it did not hurt so much. It didn't really matter if he died now, he would get to heaven. He knew his name—it was Sevim!

Sevim sat there for a long time. The dawn came, tinting the swamps with beautiful pink light, making the black waters shimmer, and lighting the vines and the weeping trees in lush shades of green. The bright colours drifted across the swamp as if some artful god was painting a swift, light stroke across the day. His long exposure might have killed him in his weakened state, but the touch of sunlight gave him just enough warmth.

Eventually the brightness of the morning faded, cooling into the late afternoon. Sevim was still beside the water, but he had curled up on his side and lain down.

His drifting thoughts began to calm. For many hours his name had whirled around his brain like some demented swamp-fly: *Sevim, Sevim, Sevim, my name is Sevim.* He had been too frightened to stop this thought. After all, he might die at any moment and Lord Rann, the god who would come to judge his soul, would demand that he know his name.

But as the shadows of the swamplands grew longer and darker, and the day began to wind down into cold dark once more, Sevim still had not died. As if from nowhere, a clear thought formed: *It had been kind of Spall to tell him.*

In spite of his childish temper tantrum, the ghost had told Sevim his name before he left. It was an act of kindness, something so rare in his life that he felt touched by it. Pushing himself upright, he looked around the darkening swamp, He half-expected to see the ghost still watching him, but there was no one to be seen.

Sevim realized for the first time that now the sun had gone he was cold, freezing cold. His teeth began to chatter and his naked flesh shuddered and ticked as his muscles tensed again. Glancing around he saw the rumpled red heap of his blanket further back up the hillside towards the Tauloc. With a tired sigh he crawled towards it, not trusting his legs to stand up. He knew that if he did not warm up soon, he would lose the battle his body was still fighting. His mind, of course, had already given up.

Once he reached the blanket, he wrapped it around himself once more, tucking it under his legs. Then, for the first time, he allowed himself to think about survival, about finding food or trying to start a fire. However, as he slowly began to get warm, he knew he was too weak and tired to move again. Sevim wondered if the gods were punishing him, by giving him the illusion of warmth. Perhaps they were allowing him to feel there might be some hope, while in fact, he was too weakened to do anything about it.

'What, still here? Don't you even know when to quit?' Spall appeared in front of the Tauloc, leaning against the stone pillar. He seemed so determined to appear casual, it was clear he had not given up on Sevim just yet. Sevim was surprised to find he felt a surge of happiness at seeing the moody ghost.

'Spall,' he said, 'don't worry. I

don't think I'll be here much longer. The crocodiles might have refused to eat me, but the cold will get me anyway.'

Spall raised his eyebrows and pouted at this. 'Can't have that. Do you know how often someone wanders into this gods-forsaken swamp? Not bloody often.' He frowned at Sevim as if the mere fact that he was annoyed could force him to get up, however weak he was. Then Spall seemed to have an idea. He pointed towards the ground near to Sevim, muttering something under his breath that sounded like a curse.

An orange flare of light lit the swamp and Sevim felt a welcome blast of heat on his face. The light dazzled him for a moment, making his eyes water. When he blinked the tears away, he saw a small fire just a few yards away from where he sat. Spall had managed to set one of the hillocks of swamp-grass ablaze.

Sevim gave an amazed chuckle.

'Th-thank-you,' he began, edging closer to the heat.

'Yeah. Don't get carried away. You'll have to put some sticks on it or something to keep it going,' Spall shrugged. He seemed faintly embarrassed by Sevim's joy. 'I can't pick things up, you know, being a ghost and all.'

Sevim did not reply but began to pick up twigs and dried vines near where he sat, to throw onto the fire. After a few minutes it was crackling and giving out a steady heat. Encouraged by this, Sevim made the effort to stand up and cleared an area around the fire by pulling up the swamp-grass, to make sure it would not spread. The activity warmed his tired bones still more and he began to feel almost normal. 'How did you manage to get it started?' he asked. 'We're on such boggy ground.'

'It's rock under there,' Spall pointed, drawing an invisible line between the fire and the Tauloc. 'I knew it was rock above the building I was in.'

'How old were you when they put you in there, Spall?'

'Ten.'

'*Ten?*' Sevim was horrified.

'But I didn't die straight away. Maybe that's something we have in common, we won't give in.' He fixed Sevim with a steady gaze. 'Even if we *say* we don't care.'

'You survived, in there?'

Spall smiled grimly. 'For four years.'

'How—what did you eat? How did you . . . it would send a man insane.'

'Lucky I was just a stupid young boy then, eh? Rats mostly.'

'By the gods,' Sevim breathed. 'That was so cruel . . .'

'To be fair, the priests did expect me to die rather more quickly,' Spall said. But his tone was not bitter—he could have been discussing the weather. Sevim suspected this was an act for his benefit.

Spall, what did you do?'

'Eh?'

'What was your crime? It must have been bad.'

Spall shrugged. 'I was innocent. Unjustly accused.'

'Of what?' Sevim persisted.

'Murder. Mass murder.'

There was a slight pause as Sevim tried to think of something to say in response to this. But really, he could think of nothing. He looked at Spall again, realising he did not doubt the young ghost had been capable of murder when he was alive. It was a shock—not least because he couldn't choose his company in the swamps. Spall was the only companion he was likely to have.

Finally, he just said, 'Oh,' and nodded as if this was the sort of thing people told him every day.

Spall gave a wry chuckle at Sevim's reaction. 'Does it matter now? I got my punishment, didn't I?'

'You just said you were innocent,' Sevim reminded him. 'But you're right, all I can judge you on is *now*, and you have been very fair to me. What is it that you want, Spall? I will help you if I can.'

Spall smiled, and once again Sevim was struck by the way his smile had a worrying quality to it, like an echo of something sly.

'I need you to go down into the Tauloc and burn my body,' Spall said, and his expression was serious again. 'I have haunted this wasteland for over one hundred years. If you do this, I will be able to rest in peace.'

'You mean your ghost will vanish?'

'Yes.'

CHAPTER SIX

He peered doubtfully into the pitch-black doorway. Musty air, damp as everything else in the swamps, drifted outwards. It carried the faint, sweet scent of decay with it. The firebrand he carried flared green as it caught the marsh gases.

'So, I just go all the way to the bottom and set fire to . . . to your body?'

'Yeah. That's right,' Spall said. 'They put some things in there which could be useful to you,' he added, as if this might encourage Sevim.

'Useful?'

'Weapons, clothes, that kind of thing.'

Sevim turned back to look at the ghost, frowning. 'That seems unlikely,' he said, watching Spall's expression closely. 'They didn't *want* you to get to the afterlife, that's why they trapped you in here.'

'Well, yes. The stuff belonged to other people.' Spall sighed. 'My victims, if you must know. The weapons were the ones *they claimed* I used to kill people.'

'Oh.'

'Look, it's *not true*, all right. I was innocent.'

'So you said.' Sevim adjusted his blanket. He had managed to tear a hole in the centre of it so that he could wear it like a loose cloak. He had to admit he was attracted by the idea of having proper clothes to wear and perhaps a sword or arrows to hunt with. It made him feel as if he could really survive and leave the swamps forever.

'All right, Spall.' He took his first step inside the Tauloc, and the flickering light of his firebrand threw shadows onto the slick blackness of the walls. 'Are you coming with me?'

'I'll follow on.'

Sevim wasn't surprised the ghost

was unwilling to go with him. After all, *he* wouldn't like to look at his own corpse. A few yards inside the door a long spiral stairway began. The uneven rock of the stairs was slippery with green moss, so Sevim started to descend slowly, placing his bare feet carefully. All around him the walls of the Tauloc were covered with carvings, symbols and writing in some strange language. The uneasy thought drifted through his mind that the Shemari priests had gone to a lot of trouble to make sure Spall's spirit was trapped and would never escape, or enter heaven.

It was quiet down here, an airless, muffled kind of quiet, except for the tiny high sounds of water dripping down the walls. Sevim's firebrand also made an occasional hiss or crackle as it flared in the marsh gases. He began to worry about it going out and leaving him down here in the dark, and felt a pang of sympathy for Spall. The ghost had been just a young boy and must have been so afraid when they left him.

Sevim glanced back up the stairs. He had come a long way down already and could no longer make out any gleam of moonlight from the open doorway. A sudden sound made him jump, a fast scuttling sound, and he remembered what Spall had said about eating the rats. But it sounded like something bigger than a rat. He paused to gather his wits before continuing down. Surely he must be nearing the bottom soon.

But still the stairs continued to spiral downward. Although Spall had taken his pain away again Sevim grew tired from carrying the flaming torch. The muscles beneath his arm and around his ribcage were badly bruised and now he struggled to hold his burden aloft. As he had to steady himself against the wall on his right side, he could not switch the weight into his other hand. He began to wonder if he should stop for a short rest. Then as he rounded the next turn of the stair, he met a sight which almost froze the blood in his veins.

Something—some creature—was crouching in the darkness ahead of him. It was huge, bigger than a man, but covered in filthy scales, which glinted in dark blood red. Its face was a repulsive mixture of snake and rodent. As soon as the flicker of his torch touched upon it, the creature raised its head and snarled at Sevim, the light catching sharp fangs, dripping with long strands of bloody saliva. The sound it made was a harsh hiss, and a blast of stinking air carried towards him. The creature discarded the rat it had been tearing apart. Then it dropped onto four spindly legs and started to move towards Sevim, as if to pursue him.

With a yell of fright, he turned on his heel and ran back up the stairway without stopping to look back. Forgetting to be careful on the steps he slipped and crashed to his knees but got back up and kept running. His breath came in loud gasps which echoed around the fathomless space of the Tauloc.

He didn't know how far he had gone before he realised the creature was not coming up the stairwell behind him. Trying to control his ragged breathing, he stopped and bent double, dropping the torch in order to hold onto his ribs.

'Oh, I wouldn't do that if I were you. Fire's the only thing they're afraid of.' Spall's ghostly form wavered a few stairs above him, his face a picture of innocent concern.

'They?' Sevim hissed. *'They*—you mean there's more? What in Rann's hell was that thing?'

The young spirit at least had the grace to look shame-faced. 'That's a *yalik*. They're a joining of other creatures—well, dead creatures really. They are the Guardians of this Tauloc.'

'The Shemari certainly went to a

lot of trouble over you,' Sevim frowned. 'Well, that's it then. There's no way I can get down there.' He started wearily up the next set of steps.

'What? No, wait. You can't give up that easily! Remember, there's clothes and weapons down there. And you've got fire—that's all you need to keep them at bay.'

Sevim considered this for a moment. 'How many?' he asked. 'And *don't* lie to me!'

'A few. They're on different levels, so you'll only see one at a time.'

'Oh well, that's all right then,' Sevim could not stop the angry sarcasm creeping into his voice.

'What's the worst that can happen?' Spall argued. 'They can kill you, right? But then, you'd be no worse off than when I found you in the swamp.'

Despite his annoyance, Sevim had already turned round to snatch up the fire-brand from the floor where he had dropped it. He glared at Spall and thrust his face up close to the ghost's own. 'Oh yes, I would,' he hissed. 'Because then I'd have to spend eternity trapped here with *you*.'

He didn't wait for Spall to answer but began to go back down the stairwell again. This time he held the fire before him, like a weapon rather than just a lamp. Spall watched him go, a satisfied smirk on his face.

*   *   *

The *yalik* creature had not followed him from the level where he had first met it. Possibly it had a very short memory-span, like the animals it had been created from, and had gone back to its meal. He thought he heard a muffled sound from somewhere below. It reminded him of the hiss of a rattlesnake.

Sevim realised that he had begun to want to survive again. And it wasn't just because he didn't want to spend eternity trapped with Spall. The instinct for survival was stronger than he could have imagined.

He came to the level where he had found the creature. He could tell because there was a smear of blood on the wall where it had dashed out the brains of the rat it had been eating. The flicker of the torch showed it was still wet and fresh, but there was no sign of the beast. Perhaps the *yalik* had moved deeper into the Tauloc.

Just at that moment, without warning, something grabbed Sevim by the throat, yanking him backwards off his feet. He had only enough breath to yell once before the claws of the *yalik*, which had been hiding in the shadows, began to close around his neck, crushing his windpipe. Sevim was lifted into the air, kicking and thrashing, and the blackness of the shadows crowded in around him as he fought to stay conscious.

CHAPTER SEVEN

Just for once, luck was on Sevim's side. As he flailed his arms in panic, the burning torch came into contact with the *yalik's* head. With a snarl of rage, it dropped him suddenly on the floor, where he lay gasping. But something bad had happened to his throat. It was difficult for him to breathe, as if he could take in only a tiny amount of air at a time. With a strangled groan, Sevim pulled himself forward onto his knees to crawl into the darkness at the turn of the stairs.

There was a strange sound behind him. Swiftly, he turned back to face his attacker. He had actually set the beast ablaze. Between its scales were coarse hairs and there were enough scabby patches on its limbs and the side of its head for it to catch fire. The *yalik* was whirling around and screeching, distracted from its prey by pain and fear. Seizing his chance, Sevim lunged back to pick up the firebrand again. He pulled himself to his feet, and broke, into a lurching run to make his escape back into the stairwell.

He kept moving as quickly as he could, stopping only briefly to touch his hand to his throat, checking his injury. Breathing was still difficult and a hot, tight feeling was building in his chest. The force of the creature's grip had crushed his vocal cords. He tried coughing to see if that would help, but it made little difference. It was the type of injury that brought tears to your eyes. Sevim ignored the tears, so that they slid down his dirty cheeks unchecked.

Behind him, he could hear the sounds of the burning *yalik* as it thrashed and roared in increasing fear and pain. Smoke was beginning to drift down the stairwell and the sharp smell of burning meat followed. It was clear the Tauloc would soon have one less guardian.

The fire from the burning torch was not enough to warm him and Sevim's feet and legs were still numb with cold, which made running difficult. He could not feel the rock under his feet and kept moving only by instinct. As he rounded the next bend he saw another *yalik* ahead of him. It was smaller than the other one, and at first, it looked like an over-sized wolf.

He felt bolder now that he had beaten the first *yalik*. He thrust the firebrand towards the second, making a *shoo-ing* sound which came from his mangled throat with a strange rasping noise. The wolf turned its head towards him, and his heart skipped a beat in alarm.It began a low, vicious growling and scuttled out of the shadows towards him. Sevim could see now that it had been magically fused with a massive spider. Where its legs should have started, black spindly limbs jutted out at sharp angles, casting frightening shadows which danced in the light of the firebrand. Sevim drew back, disgusted. He had always hated spiders, since he was a young child. But he also felt something like pity for the strange creature. He wondered if it remembered being a wolf, running free with its pack, before a Shemari priest captured it.

But there was no time for Sevim to pursue this thought. The wolf *yalik* was standing right before him, its teeth bared in a vicious snarl, its ears lying flat against its skull. There could be no room for sympathy. He thrust the firebrand forward again, and the wolf backed away. Crouching forward and holding the flames as near to the wolf as he dared, Sevim began to circle slowly around towards the stairwell. The wolf turned with him, its spider legs making a heavy scratching sound on

51

the stone floor.

Not daring to take his eyes off the creature, Sevim reached out with his free hand to feel for the wall of the stairwell. Then, slowly, holding his breath, he slid his foot backwards, trying to find the edge of the stairs. He began to back down, his hand against the rough wetness of the wall to steady himself.

As Sevim backed away and the fire grew less of a threat, the wolf scuttled across the small landing again. It stood at the top of the stairs looking down at the vanishing light. Its growls echoed after Sevim, filling the space of the stairwell with threatening sound. But it made no move to pursue him and, after he cleared the next bend, Sevim risked turning around to look where he was going, his nerves still jangling. He was still listening for the tell-tale sound of the strange creature's eight legs, tip-tapping on the stonework behind him. In the distance, up another level, he could still hear the shrieks of the first *yalik* as it died, consumed by flames. He felt guilty about that somehow.

His torch guttered suddenly, as if it had been caught by a draught. The light dipped almost into blackness for a few anxious moments before the flames recovered. Sevim's mouth went dry with fear. Without the precious fire he would be unable to fulfil his promise to Spall. More importantly, he would be unable to pass the guardians again and escape. He would be a prisoner of the Tauloc too. He was thinking this as he lost his footing and fell.

*   *   *

The ghost was still waiting by the main entrance, pacing back and forth, his lips moving as if he was having an argument with himself— which he was.

'It's too much,' Spall muttered. ' I

should have told him. Why would anyone do it? It's too much to ask. Lying is bad, bad, bad. But no one can punish me now. No one . . .' A sly smile flitted across the ghost's elegant face and for a moment, he looked almost happy. His happiness was cut short however, when he heard a shout of alarm from inside the Tauloc.

'Sevim?' Spall turned towards the top of the stairs again, but stopped. He hated going down there. He had been so long in the dark and the quiet. But at least the sound seemed to be coming from deep inside the buried tower. Perhaps Sevim was nearing the grave chamber.

With a sigh, Spall vanished.

*　　　*　　　*

Sevim was always one to count his blessings—in a cynical sort of a way. So as he stared horrified at the way his foot was twisted around, he decided that it was a *good* thing he was completely numb with cold. At least he couldn't feel any pain.

Then a weak flickering light distracted him—the firebrand! It lay on the damp stone floor some distance away and it was struggling to stay alight. There were no flames now, just a glow at its centre. In a few moments it would go out and the Tauloc would return to darkness.

It was tempting to simply stay where he was and watch the fire die. But Sevim felt strangely committed to his task now, not for Spall's sake, but his own. He realised he had fallen as far as he could go: he was at the base of the tower. Behind the next bend, still hidden in deep shadow, must be the door which led to Spall's burial chamber. And in there, were clothes and weapons.

Sevim was beyond exhaustion now. He pulled himself forward on his hands and knees to rescue the precious fire. Picking it up, he stared into the orange warmth at its heart. He could feel the heat dance across his face like a welcome touch of grace. Although his throat was still painful, he blew gently onto the fire as if returning its favour.

After a few moments rest, he struggled to his feet, wincing at the pain of his damaged ankle. He re-adjusted his weight onto the other leg, then he hobbled forward and pushed open the heavy door of the burial chamber.

CHAPTER EIGHT

Everywhere the light touched was gold, or so it seemed to Sevim. A huge treasure lay before him: statues, caskets, candelabras and jewels were scattered across the floor. They glinted in the light from his firebrand—the first light the burial chamber had known since it was sealed.

As he realised this, Sevim turned back to look at the doorway. There was no sign of forced entry, no broken wood to show it had been kicked open. He frowned. Surely a treasure this vast would have been locked away?

He turned back to limp further into the space. There was an archway ahead of him which led into an antechamber. This might be where Spall's body lay. Sevim cleared a way through the scattered treasure. It was no use to him anyway. The promised clothes and weapons were nowhere to be seen.

Inside the smaller room was a stone dais. Lying on this dais was the shape of a mummified body. It had once been a tall man, and he had a golden death mask on his face. As Sevim drew near he raised the firebrand in order to look more closely, half expecting to see Spall's fine features.

'But that's not . . .'

'Me? No.'

He looked back towards the treasure room to see Spall standing in the archway, his arms folded across his chest as if mimicking the corpse. He still had an air of bravado, but the expression on his face was deadly serious.

'I don't understand, Spall. I thought you said—'

'I lied. That's me over there.' He nodded his head in the direction of the corner of the room. Sevim moved around the dais to look.

'Oh, Spall,' he said quietly.

The heap of bones seemed incredibly small and fragile. It looked to Sevim as though the corpse (somehow he couldn't think of it being Spall) had curled up in the corner with his knees hugged up to his chest. And that's all there was, just a jumbled pile of bleached bones. Any clothes Spall might have been wearing had decayed away.

Spall seemed uncomfortable with Sevim's pity. 'It was a long time ago,' he shrugged.

'And who is he, the real prisoner of the Tauloc?'

'He was my master, Asa Varroch. Don't waste your sympathy on him either. He was evil. Really, really evil. They were right to contain him and his spirit here. He—'

'Wait—you mean, his spirit is still here?' Sevim looked around nervously but there was no sign of movement in the musty air of the room.

'Well, no actually—he kind of escaped. When I . . .' Spall looked uncomfortable. 'When I tried to rob the tomb.'

Sevim snorted. 'You robbed your own master's tomb?' he said in amazement.

'Look, you don't know what he was like—some of the things I saw. He *owed* me. He was a Sin Eater. Do you know what that is?'

'Yes, they take away people's sins to allow them to be judged after death. But what's that got to do with . . . ?'

'What do you think happens to the Sin after?'

'Well, I don't know. I suppose I kind of thought it wasn't real.'

'No, it's very real. The Sin Eater is supposed to send it back to Lord Rann, in the underworld.' Spall glanced around as he said this and dropped his voice. 'They're supposed to give it back. But Asa Varroch . . .

he never did. He used the Sin as power. He was the most powerful sorcerer that ever lived.'

'Yes,' Sevim nodded, 'I think I remember his name.' He looked back at the gold death mask which seemed ironically serene and peaceful. 'So, you . . . you are responsible for letting the spirit of this monster loose in the world again?'

Spall nodded unhappily. 'But if it's any consolation, I got my just reward. Asa Varroch guessed what I would do. In fact, I think he planted the suggestion in my mind. Not that I'm excusing my actions,' he added hastily. 'When I came in here, his spirit was waiting for me. He bound me to the Tauloc to take his place, so that the gods would not notice his absence. I was trapped here, still alive for the first while, and then as a ghost.'

Sevim sighed heavily and began to hobble back into the treasure chamber. 'Wait! Where are you going?' Spall called out in alarm.

'I'm looking for something to scoop water out of that puddle,' Sevim replied, his voice still cracked and hoarse. 'Do carry on justifying what you and your miserable master did, though, won't you? I'm still listening.'

Spall did not rise to this sarcasm. 'I'm trying to make amends. I've waited many, many years for a living person to come and assist me. I need to bring him back here. Trap him as the Shemari intended.'

'Freeing your spirit in the process, I'm guessing.' Sevim came back into the chamber using an ornamental gold staff as a crutch and carrying a small gilded bowl. Spall took a step back at the sight of the staff, but did not comment on it.

'It doesn't matter what you think of me, not really. But you were about to die in the swamp when I found you. Surely you can see that trapping

Asa Varroch is for the greater good.'

Sevim had sat down on the floor at the end of the tomb. He sipped gratefully at the cold water he scooped from the puddle. He doubted his throat would ever feel the same, but at least the water numbed it slightly. For some reason, the memory of Kalia drifted through his mind. He thought of the way she had looked on that evening, the way she had smiled at him as she spoke his name. He could hear her voice now, to go with the memory: *Sevim*. Spall had at least given him his name back.

'All right, so you need me to set fire to this place. Then that will draw his spirit back here?'

'Yes.'

'For the greater good of mankind—of people.'

'Yes,' Spall frowned.

Sevim took another sip of his water. 'No,' he said. 'I won't do it. People deserve everything they get in my opinion.'

CHAPTER NINE

'What?'

'You don't know much about me, do you Spall? Look at me.' Sevim spoke calmly but the bitterness in his words was clear. 'Do you think I've had a happy life? Do you think mankind has been kind to someone who looks like me?'

'But that's not everyone, Sevim.'

'Maybe not, but everyone in my experience.' Sevim sniffed. 'I'll just die here I guess and then you'll have company for eternity.'

'Oh for godssakes. It's that girl isn't it, she really upset you? Look, maybe you don't know everything about her.' Without further explanation, Spall walked swiftly over to where Sevim was sitting and touched his forehead with his middle finger, muttering a word under his breath that Sevim could not understand.

'What are you . . . ?' But before he could protest, Sevim blacked out. He slumped forward, and the little golden water bowl fell from his loose fingers to clang on the floor.

'Sweet dreams,' Spall whispered.

He was back. Spall had somehow sent him back to the earthy warmth of his little cave in the hillside. A fire was burning in the grate, crackling the kindling he had just added.

Outside, it was still raining, that same storm. Sevim knew immediately he was back in his dream and it was the same night—the night that Kalia had visited him, and been kind to him, just for the sake of a bet. He knew this because he was still sitting slumped on the ground with his back to the door, and he was crying. But it was not just because of Kalia and her friends. Their stupidity had opened the floodgates of grief for his mother and father, who had been dead for only a few months

*when he met Kalia. Since their deaths,
Sevim had been truly alone. Now
Kalia and her friends had reminded
him of this.*

'Get up.'

*He wiped his nose on his sleeve and
looked around him, bleary-eyed.
'Huh?' The voice he heard was inside
his head.*

*'Get up and follow her. Hurry up.
We don't have all night.'*

*Sevim thought he knew the voice but
could not place it. For some reason he
felt he had to do as it commanded.
Flinging open the door, he dashed out
into the pouring rain in the direction
Kalia had gone. As his splashing
footsteps brought him closer and closer
to the courtyard of Kalia's home,
Sevim began to doubt what he was
doing. This was not what really
happened . . . not what he had done
that night.*

*As he reached the side of the
building, Sevim pressed against the
wall, sheltering beneath the bronze*

dragons on the eaves. Like most houses in Chasia, the windows had no glass and were protected only by slatted wooden shutters. Keeping still as some white statue, he could hear the voices of the girls who had offended him. They sounded breathless, having just run in from the storm. Some of them were still laughing and joking. Sevim flinging the heavy crock at them had done little to affect their mood.

Kalia's voice cut across his thoughts. She was standing nearest the window. 'No, no Tayna, I don't think it's funny.' Her tone was sharp, as if her friends had pushed her beyond the limits of her usual good nature.

'Oh, come on Kalia,' someone said. 'You must admit it was pretty funny when—'

'No. Listen to me. What we did tonight was beneath us. That young man has just lost his parents. He's struggling to survive and yet he turned up at my father's hiring line this morning. And he did a full day's work.

67

I'll bet he hasn't eaten for a few days.'

There was a short silence before someone remarked, 'Maybe he shouldn't have chucked the stew at us then.' This was followed by giggles but Kalia was unmoved.

'Tomorrow morning, I'm going to apologise to Sevim, and you can all come with me.' When the other girls protested, Kalia added firmly, 'or you're not coming to my party.'

Sevim could scarcely believe it. He found himself grinning like some demented fool standing out there in the rain. Of course, they never had come to apologise. The other girls must have persuaded Kalia to change her mind. But that didn't matter. She—Kalia—had fought his corner!

But there was no time to revel in this idea. Sevim was yanked back to the present and to reality with a click of Spall's fingers. He opened his eyes, the smile dying away as he realised where he was.

'Or this,' Spall said, touching Sevim's forehead again. 'Do you remember this?'

Sevim knew at once where this memory came from: he had just been beaten half to death by Kalia's own father and a mob of ignorant villagers.

'No,' *he moaned out loud.* 'Spall, not this, I . . .

'Get up. Get up. They can't see you. You and I are just 'visiting' the past' Look.'

'At what?'

'Look in the doorway.'

Sevim did as Spall told him; now he found it easy to float away from his body. At least the pain stopped.

He saw her straight away. She was slumped to the ground in the doorway and she was weeping, big wracking sobs. Her face was wet with tears and mucus where her nose had run; her eyes were red and puffy, her hair sticking to her cheek. He thought she was the most beautiful thing he had ever seen . . .

And then, things kind of skip forward
. . . things dreamt and things remembered . . .

He was sitting on bare ground in the mud and the rain, numb with shock, and she gave him the blanket. Only she didn't just hand it to him, she wrapped it around his cold shoulders. As she did so, she gave the blanket a little tug to pull it around him and it was like a tiny hug. She said nothing but the compassion in her eyes was enough.

Another click of Spall's fingers and Sevim was back to the stark, grey reality of the Tauloc. He looked at Spall for a long moment, a curious expression of relief on his face.
'Thank you,' he said.

CHAPTER TEN

'Are we ready?' Sevim's hand shook as he held the firebrand above the corpse of Asa Varroch.

Spall licked his lips nervously. 'Sevim, you do know he's likely to kill you?'

But Sevim just smiled in response. He had a new and stronger belief in himself now. 'Yes,' he said. Then he touched the firebrand to the corpse.

They had found some pitch behind the dais, probably left there by the priest who had made the final enchanted seals. Of course it had dried many years before into a solid block of tar. Sevim had shattered this over the body of Asa Varroch like blackened confetti. In less than a minute the flames began to take hold. Thankfully, the thick smoke was drawn upwards by cold air into some unseen vent, at least at first.

The Tauloc was uncannily quiet for a while; only the crackling of the flames could be heard. After a few minutes Sevim turned to speak to Spall.

'Are you sure—'

But before he could finish, an unearthly sound began: a wind, a tornado, wailing and shrieking through the swamp. It was as if the whole of the swamp outside was being lifted into the air and torn apart—the water, the trees, everything. Then there was a BANG, and the whole Tauloc shook to its foundations. Sevim and Spall stared at each other in fright.

Another BANG, as though some giant evil child had swiped at the tower and was now gripping the Tauloc in its fist, attempting to pull it from its foundations.

The third bang caused such a vibration that Sevim was knocked from his feet. By the time he pulled himself upright again, a thin, almost gaunt figure was standing amongst the smoke, glaring towards him. Spall was nowhere to be seen. He was probably hidden by the plume of smoke rising from the body.

Asa Varroch was old, but he was still the most frightening person Sevim had ever seen. Power flowed from him, dark, energetic power. He wore grey robes, which seemed to swirl around his body like the smoke that now surrounded him.

'Who are you?' he frowned. He did not wait for a reply but reached out a long skinny arm towards Sevim, his fingers curled like claws. It seemed some invisible force flowed from his hand, for Sevim felt himself pulled forward as if something had grabbed hold of his tatty blanket. His feet were no longer touching the floor. In an instant, he was nose to nose with the imposing figure of Asa Varroch.

Suddenly he could see Spall. The ghost had recovered from his shock and was standing behind his former master making strange hand motions. Sevim was too shocked to realise the gestures meant, *keep him talking!*

But something had happened to Sevim. He was committed to his course of action now, and he felt strangely alive. Staring the wizard directly in the eyes he said calmly, 'I have come to re-capture your soul, Asa Varroch.' He was dimly aware of Spall's shocked expression.

Asa Varroch's lip curled in a sneer. The smoke from the burning corpse began to whirl around the chamber walls in echo of the storm the wizard had created outside the Tauloc. The floor of the chamber seemed to fall away so that they were suspended, floating in a black, spiralling chaos. Sevim expected the wizard to throw back his head and laugh at his pitiful situation, but he did not. Instead, with his other hand, he simply touched Sevim's face with wide spread fingers. Sevim screamed. He could feel the life being torn out of his body, ripped painfully from his bruised and beaten flesh.

'Spaaalllll!'

The sorcerer blinked sharply, his attention distracted by Sevim screaming aloud the name of his own disobedient servant. He halted, looking round, but still held tightly to Sevin. The boy's death was surely just delayed.

'Spall? What have you done now, you troublesome little maggot?' Asa Varroch roared. 'Come and face your master!'

For the moment, Spall had no such intention. A thin trail of yellow-gold light had begun to form, snaking out from beneath the burning remains of the body, not smoke, not fire, something *other*. Its snake-like energy was seeking the wizard, the victim that the Shemari priests had intended it to capture and bind. As he turned towards his own burning remains, Asa Varroch also saw the golden coil of light. He gave a snarl of rage. 'Make it stop, Spall. I *will* kill your friend and keep his soul.'

Spall stepped out into the storm, his white robes and pale blonde hair snapping and billowing in the wind which still blew through the chamber. 'Let him go, master,' he said. 'For three centuries you have escaped the justice of the gods. You have held on to what you owe them. But it's over.'

He was trying to distract Asa Varroch, and for a moment, it seemed the old man was fooled. Then he reacted. Turning back to Sevim, he reached out once more, making a pulling and twisting motion with his hands. Sevim's pitiful screams were thankfully lost in the wail of the storm.

Spall could not stand Sevim's agony—it was so unjust. With a yell of outrage, he leapt towards Sevim's helpless form, grabbing him into a tight bear hug and pulling him away from Asa Varroch's deathly grip.

There was a sound like the ending of the world.

A flash of golden light.

And then, merciful, silent, black.

CHAPTER ELEVEN

The first thing Sevim became aware of was the smell of herbs, burning herbs: sage, laurel, and maybe feverfew. He had a vague thought that perhaps Spall was trying to waken him.

But when he did wake up, he was not lying on a bed or even a floor, in fact he wasn't lying down at all. He was moving around, almost *dancing*. And he was distant, distant from the world somehow, as if he was looking at it through someone else's eyes.

Fighting panic, he looked down at his hands—except they were *not his hands*. They were holding huge feathers, wafting the scented herbal smoke around the room.

What—what's happening to me?

Sevim? Sevim—is that you?' It was Spall's voice, inside his head. *'You're back! Praise the gods, I had given you*

78

up. No—calm down—breathe— breathe . . .

'I'm sorry. I need to take a break. I will meditate and return to you soon. I know your time is short, my lord, but your sins are heavy.' This last comment was spoken aloud and addressed to an elderly man who was lying on a bed in the smoke filled room.

Dear gods. That's not me is it? Am I old now—am I dying?

No, just wait. Wait. I can explain everything.

Spall?

Yes, it's me, Spall.

*   *   *

He is moving, walking across the room, and he is going outside. He feels a surge of joy at the sight of a clear blue sky in which swallows are swooping and calling. It is a beautiful day.

He carries on walking until he

reaches a small temple building. It is whitewashed and plain with only the symbol of Imeris, the god of healing, painted outside by the door. Entering the simple little chapel, he sits down on a wooden bench. He keeps looking at his own hands: he cannot believe how delicate and pink-looking they are . . .

We don't have long, Sevim. Now's not a good time to explain.

' *"We" don't have long? We? What— you're inside my head now? Forever?*

Not exactly. Not at this moment. You're in mine. We're . . .

Yes?

We're sharing this body.

Uh-huh.

Sometimes it will be me, Spall. But not very often now you're back, I'm guessing. And sometimes it will be you, Sevim.

There is a short silence while Sevim tries to take this in.

Sevim, are you still there? I know it's a shock.

Yes. So I can physically change back to me?

Yes, you can. Look, I'm sorry Sevim, it was all I could do. I couldn't let Asa Varroch take you like that. You would have been trapped with him, inside that stone tomb.

They both shuddered.

But I'm afraid that's not all, Spall's voice went on. *Something of his spirit must have got mixed up with our new form. We've taken on Asa Varroch's mission. We've become a Sin Eater. Sevim, you won't like it. It's . . . kind of horrible.*

Well, we don't have to do it, do we? Sevim asked. *We can just go away.*

No, it's not that simple. Trust me. When the Shemari priests summon us, we have to go. We are bound to obey them.

Ach, how bad can it be? Sevim smiled. *At least he thought he smiled—he wasn't sure if his body obliged.*

It was very bad: their first client had a whole lot of sin.

The atmosphere within the room was cramped and airless, a situation made worse by the presence of three Shemari priests. They were expecting the elderly land-owner to sign a large amount of his wealth over to the church before he died. The old man would not do so until he was made pure again. That was where Spall came in.

The magic was simple. In fact, because they had inherited Asa Varroch's dark talents, it was instinctive. But Spall took his time, chanting and dancing and wafting the disease-tainted air. Eventually, there was a bright flash of white light and something that looked like a bubble made from slimy, muddy water burst out of the man's mouth. It hung suspended in the air, polluting the room until it dried into a thin, papery film.

You might want to close your eyes, Spall whispered.

He proceeded to eat the Sin.

*   *   *

Sickened and appalled, Sevim was glad to return home. He was even more glad when he saw he was near the outskirts of his old village, and Spall had managed to find his cave dwelling.

As they came through the door, the weariness of the world seemed to crash upon Sevim's mind. He fell onto his dingy little bed as if it were the finest feather mattress. And as he drifted off to sleep he became aware of a warm tingling sensation in his body. Lifting his hand before his face he wasn't entirely surprised to see his own familiar white flesh once more. Spall, it seemed, was as good as his word and allowed Sevim possession of their shared body.

'Welcome home, Sevim,' he muttered.

*   *   *

He was wakened by someone tapping on his door. He went to open it still sleepy and naked, his hair tousled and his cover wrapped around him.

It was Kalia. She drew back as the door opened, still afraid that he might touch her.

'Oh. Good evening, Miss.'

She managed an uncertain smile. 'I heard you were back, Sevim, and that you have a new calling now. I just wanted to . . . to wish you luck with it.'

'Th-thank-you, Miss Kalia.'

'It sounds like you need some honey for that throat. I'll have one of the Shemari bring some over. Bye.'

*   *   *

84

She turned to hurry back towards the safety of the village and Sevim watched her go, the sunlight making her red hair glow like some beautiful beacon of hope.

Don't get carried away, Spall's voice warned him, sensing his pleasure. *I'm guessing her father sent her to sweeten you up after the beating. He must be worried you'll have him arrested.*

Sevim shrugged. *Yes, I know. It's just good to see her again, that's all. Seems we're more important now,'* he thought. He was already becoming used to sending his thoughts to Spall.

Yes. And it's good that we're here. Some day soon, Sevim, Kalia is going to need you.

*   *   *

Sevim didn't feel the need to ask why or when she might need him, as he would be here anyway. He turned back into his little cave. Its brown and green hues were touched by the kindness of the morning sun, so it looked warmer and more welcoming than he had ever noticed before.

*   *   *

He would be here. In the meantime, at least he was no longer alone.

He would never be alone again.